SANTA CLAWS

The Christmas Crab

Priscilla Cummings

illustrated by

Marcy Dunn Ramsey

 Tidewater Publishers
Centreville, Maryland

The waves turned to ice and the snow fell all day
One cold Christmas Eve in the Chesapeake Bay.
Ashore, colored lights lit the tree in the square
And carolers sang, music filling the air.
The stockings were hung and the cocoa was hot.
Good children said prayers, but sleep they could not!

Meanwhile, outside of town, in a cove dusted white
All the animals had a much quieter night.
The herons and egrets, the ducks and the geese,
Found refuge together, and nestled in peace.
Furry foxes and raccoons and tiny gray moles
Were curled up asleep in their dens and their holes.
While below the bay's ice crust, all tucked in their beds
The oysters and crabs and fish rested their heads.
Not once would they move — not a peep from the deep —
Until the spring sun woke them all from their sleep.

But suddenly noise cut the cold air in half!
Then faintly, so faintly, the tiniest laugh . . .
No, this Christmas Eve in the Chesapeake Bay
Was not going to pass in a typical way,
For below in the water, awake in the mud,
Was a naughty young crab the others called Spud.

Spud hated to nap. He was just like his father.
He thought all that sleep was a waste and a bother.
Jumping out of the mud he gave others a poke.
A poke and a poke until all of them woke.
"Get up, crabs!" Spud hollered. "Don't lie there and snooze!
Just think of the time you waste, time that you lose!"

He grabbed a tin can
where he'd hidden some clothes
Then stuck a plump berry on his face for a nose.
A sock that he'd found made a grand Santa hat
And a waterman's glove made his thin legs look fat.
Some whiskers he'd cut from grass stored in the fall
And eight rubber boots on eight feet made him tall.

A crab dressed as Santa — a Santa with claws!
If you met this Santa, would you know who it was?
He winked and he chuckled. His pincers went click!
Why, no one would guess this crab wasn't St. Nick!

"I'm off!" Spud cried gaily, a grin eye to eye.
He swam away sideways. His claw waved good-bye.
By then crabs were wide-eyed and giggling, too.
They could not believe what they saw young Spud do.

He thumped on the oysters. He pulled the fish tails!
Ignoring their moaning and groaning and wails.
"I'm Santa with Claws!" Spud yelled. "Santa who pinches!
Get up or I'll pinch you, you little fish grinches!"
"Oh, what for?" a perch begged him. A crab wondered, too.
"If we get up for Christmas, then what will we do?"
"You'll see," Spud declared. "I have a surprise.
Get up now. Be patient. Don't open your eyes!"

Spud swam away quickly to wake up the band,
A group of musicians who played in the sand.
A fiddler crab trio, a flounder on flute,
An eel with a sax and a bass with a lute.
The band had a lovely young rockfish on harp
And French horns were blown by both catfish and carp.
The jellyfish blobbed while a ray practiced drumming
The crab chorus gathered and warmed up by humming.
The Bay Bottom Band — every gill, every fin —
Was ready to play when Spud called out, "Begin!"
The music was loud. Oysters popped open shells,
In time with the rhythm, they sounded like bells.
With all of that singing and dancing and clapping
Not one single creature remained in bed napping!

Spud used things he'd found for a fine Christmas tree
Then strung up green seaweed and shells carefully
An old sunken rowboat provided a spot
For Spud to place foods that were tasty and hot.
He hugged each dear friend and said, "Now, don't you see?
Why Christmas awake once meant so much to me!"

Their talking and laughing made so many bubbles
At first no one heard that Real Santa had troubles.
But when they heard BOOM! Which was followed by WHACK!
They gazed up to see the ice tremble and crack.

Real Santa called "Help!" as his sleigh circled twice
Before trying to land once again on the ice.
"Oh, gosh," moaned real Santa. "A storm without warning!
And all these fine toys to hand out before morning!"
The snow finally stopped and stars brightened the night.
But Santa was lost. It was such a sad sight.

'Twas Spud who spoke up: "I can show you the way!
I know every inch of the Chesapeake Bay!"
Real Santa was startled. "Are you Santa, too?"
Spud chuckled, "Well, yeah. But not
a real one like you!"

Real Santa said, "Fine! Mister Crab, have a seat!
Please show us the way. I've a deadline to meet!"
Spud pointed his claw. "The town's there, in the west.
Straight on, tell the reindeer. We'll hope for the best!"
The reindeer plunged forward in snow to their knees,
Then leapt in the air with astonishing ease.

The fish and crabs wondered: Would Spud be all right?
So high in the sky? Out of water? At night?
Afraid, they peeked over the ice toward the shore
And witnessed a sight they'd only heard of before.

A sleigh with eight reindeer flew down from the sky
And landed on rooftops of houses nearby.
Real Santa Claus, holding a sack and a light
Then jumped in each chimney and slid out of sight!
"He's just like a sand crab," one fish told his brother.
"He ducks down one hole, then he scoots down another!"

The fish and crabs waited and worried and shivered
While all of the toys and the gifts were delivered.
"Hooray!" they cheered Spud. Santa thanked his crab guide.
"I wish there was one Christmas gift left," he sighed.